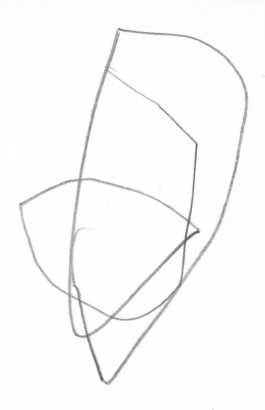

I'm Going to Build a Supermarket One of These Days

New York, Toronto, London, Sydney

I'm going to BUILD a SUPER MARKET one of these days

by Helen Baten and Barbara von Molnar
adapted by Bill Martin, Jr.
with pictures by Papas

Copyright © 1970 by Holt, Rinehart and Winston, Inc.
Published Simultaneously in Canada
Printed in the United States of America
Library of Cong. No: 70-109209
ISBN: 0-03-084595-5

HOLT, RINEHART AND WINSTON, INC.

a Bill Martin Instant Reader

I'm going to build a supermarket one of these days,

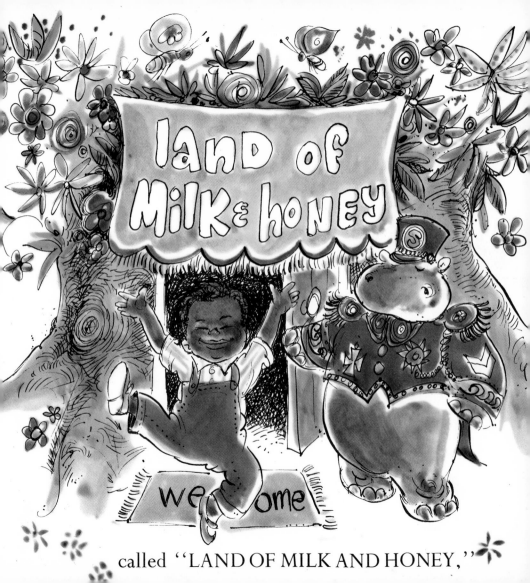

called "LAND OF MILK AND HONEY,"

Where every shelf says  HELP YOURSELF!

I'm going to build a supermarket one of these days,
where adults are not admitted,

Where you roller-skate through the entrance gate,

and racing is permitted...

Where elephants wave the welcome flags . . .

Where kangaroos serve as shopping bags...

Where the piped-in music has a holiday sound...?

Where you meet your friends on a merry-go-round...

Where the alphabet soup always spells your name...

Where you take time out for a baseball game...

Where a marshmallow bear is spinning cotton candy...

Where revolving shelves keep the ice cream handy...

Where coconut cakes wear a wreath of candles...

Where watermelon comes with juice-proof handles...

Where chickens lay Easter eggs, fancily dyed...

Where boxes of doughnuts are licorice tied...

Where you use the biggest grapefruit
for a game of catch-the-bouncers . . .

Where you see the latest movies
underneath the checkout counters . . .

Where you do target practice shooting holes in the cheese . . .

Where the fun never ends, stay as long as you please...

George

fred

Mary

And when I build my supermarket
one fine day,

I'll be sending you
an airmail invitation...

...to come and shop with me, it's absolutely free...

at my market with the SUPERreputation!